THE BOY FROM THE DRAGON PALACE

A Folktale from Japan

Retold by
Margaret Read MacDonald

Illustrated by
Sachiko Yoshikawa

ALBERT WHITMAN & COMPANY
CHICAGO, ILLINOIS

A poor flower seller found no one to buy his flowers.
So he decided to give them to the Dragon King
who lives beneath the sea.

"A gift for YOU, Dragon King!" he called.

And he tossed the flowers onto the waves.

The water began to swirl.

Suddenly a beautiful lady came up from the sea.
She held a little boy in her arms!
"A 'thank you' from the Dragon King!"

The man took the little boy.
This child had the snottiest nose you ever did see!

"What will I do with this snot-nosed boy?"

"He will bring you luck!" said the beautiful lady.
"But you must make shrimp for him every day.
Put in vinegar. Put in sugar.
He likes it like that."

And she disappeared
beneath the waves.

The man carried the boy home
and made him some shrimp.
He put in vinegar. He put in sugar.

"I just spent my last coin on shrimp for you.
If you are going to bring me luck,
you had better start now."

The little boy picked up the bowl
and "SLURRRP!" he swallowed it all.

The little boy
set down the bowl.

He snuffled his nose
on his right sleeve.

He snuffled his nose
on his left sleeve.

Then he blew his nose really hard.

"HNNNK! HNNNK! HNNNK!"

And the floor was COVERED with gold!

Now the flower seller was able to buy rice and fish for himself and more shrimp for the snot-nosed little boy!

Next day, the flower seller thought . . .
"I wonder if the snot-nosed little boy can provide other things, too?"

That night when he fed the little boy his shrimp, he said,
"This wooden hut is a very poor home.
I wish I had a larger house."

The snot-nosed little boy picked up
the bowl and ate his shrimp.

"SLURRRP!"

Then he snuffled on his right sleeve.
He snuffled on his left sleeve.

And "HNNNK! HNNNK! HNNNK!"

The house began to change . . .

The house became a PALACE!

There was rich clothing for the flower seller.
And silk cushions all about.

That night when he fed the snot-nosed little boy, he said,
"It would be nice if I had some servants to take care of this palace,
and some cooks to prepare my dinner."

"SLURRRP!"

Snuffle . . . snuffle.

"HNNNK! HNNNK! HNNNK!"

The door opened and
servants marched in!

The next night the flower seller said to the cook,
"YOU make the shrimp for the snot-nosed little boy."
The cook put in vinegar.
The cook put in sugar.
But the snot-nosed little boy refused to eat.

So the flower seller had to make the shrimp himself
and feed the snotty child.

And of course he thought of something more to ask.

"It would be wonderful if I had chests full of treasure."

"SLURRRP!"

Snuffle . . . snuffle.

"HNNNK! HNNNK! HNNNK!"

It was done.

Every night the man thought of something ELSE to ask for.

"A beautiful garden to walk in!"

"A pond with golden fish!"

"Dancers to entertain me!"

Now the flower seller had everything
he could possibly want.

Still, each day he had to go down to the market,
buy shrimp, cook it up,
and feed the snot-nosed little boy.

"What a NUISANCE this is!
I am sick of looking at this snot-nosed little child.
I am much too busy to be making shrimp for him every day.
And it is SO disgusting watching him eat!"

So the flower seller took the snot-nosed little boy out of the palace.
He set him down on the road and said,
"That's enough with your snotty nose-blowing.
Go on back to the sea where you belong."

Then he went inside and shut the gate.

The snot-nosed little boy looked at the closed door and sadly shook his head.

Then he snuffled on his right sleeve.

He snuffled on his left sleeve.

And . . . "HNNNK! HNNNK! HNNNK!"

Instantly the palace disappeared.
The garden disappeared.
There was nothing left but an old wooden hut.

And a flower seller who was VERY, VERY poor.

But down in the Dragon King's palace,
the snot-nosed little boy was slurping shrimp.
"You just can't help some humans," he muttered.

"So true. So true," said the Dragon King.
"They always want something more."

The snot-nosed little boy snuffled,
"And he never once said, 'Thank you.'"

TALE NOTES

This story is retold from "The Little Boy from the Dragon Palace" in *Ancient Tales in Modern Japan: An Anthology of Japanese Folk Tales* by Fanny Hagin Mayer (Bloomington, IN: Indiana University Press, 1985). The tale was shared by Mine Kosei of Tamana-gun, Kumamoto. This story is told throughout Japan in many variations. *The Yanagita Kunio Guide to the Japanese Folk Tale*, edited and translated by Fanny Hagin Mayer (Bloomington, IN: Indiana University Press, 1986) cites versions of this story from Hachinohe, Aomori; Iwate; Niigata; Tamana-gun, Kumamoto; Kikaijima, Kagoshima. Sometimes the story is told of a woodcutter, sometimes of a flower seller. The Dragon King is Ryūjin, the dragon god who ruled from his undersea palace of red and white coral.

For Matilda Lucy and Cordelia Skye,
who always say, "That's enough . . . thank you!"—M.R.M.

For my parents.
And with special thanks to Mikako Miyazaki.—S.Y.

MacDonald, Margaret Read, 1940-
The boy from the dragon palace : a folktale from Japan / retold by Margaret Read MacDonald ; illustrated by Sachiko Yoshikawa.
p. cm.
Summary: A magical boy grants a poor flower-seller's every wish until the greedy and ungrateful man grows tired of the boy's unpleasant behavior and sends him away.
ISBN 978-0-8075-7513-0
[1. Folklore—Japan.] I. Yoshikawa, Sachiko, ill. II. Title.
PZ8.1.M15924Boy 2011
398.20952'01—dc22
[E]
2010045965

The art is collage created using watercolor and enhanced digitally.

The design is by Nicholas Tiemersma.

For more information about Albert Whitman & Company, please visit our web site at www.albertwhitman.com.

4-15
d
c.o.